A Note to Parents

D0507015

Reading books aloud and playing word [...] [par]ents can help their children learn to read. The [...] to read stories in the **My First Hello Reader! With Flash Cards** series are designed to be enjoyed together. Six activity pages and 16 flash cards in each book help reinforce phonics, sight vocabulary, reading comprehension, and facility with language. Here are some ideas to develop your youngster's reading skills:

Reading With Your Child

- Read the story aloud to your child and look at the colorful illustrations together. Talk about the characters, setting, action, and descriptions. Help your child link the story to events in his or her own life.
- Read parts of the story and invite your child to fill in the missing parts. At first, pause to let your child "read" important last words in a line. Gradually, let your child supply more and more words or phrases. Then take turns reading every other line until your child can read the book independently.

Enjoying the Activity Pages

- Treat each activity as a game to be played for fun. Allow plenty of time to play.
- Read the introductory information aloud and make sure your child understands the directions.

Using the Flash Cards

- Read the words aloud with your child. Talk about the letters and sounds and meanings.
- Match the words on the flash cards with the words in the story.
- Help your child find words that begin with the same letter and sound, words that rhyme, and words with the same ending sound.
- Challenge your child to put flash cards together to make sentences from the story and create new sentences.

Above all else, make reading time together a fun time. Show your child that reading is a pleasant and meaningful activity. Be generous with your praise and know that, as your child's first and most important teacher, you are contributing immensely to his or her command of the printed word.

—Tina Thoburn, Ed.D.
Educational Consultant

No part of this publication may be reproduced in whole or in part, or stored in a retrieval system, or transmitted in any form or by any means, electronic, mechanical, photo-copying, recording, or otherwise, without written permission of the publisher. For information regarding permission, write to Scholastic Inc., 730 Broadway, New York, NY 10003.

Library of Congress Cataloging-in-Publication Data

Packard, Mary.
    My messy room / by Mary Packard ; illustrated by Stephanie Britt.
        p.   cm.
    Summary: A stubborn young girl describes how she likes to keep her room very messy.
    ISBN 0-590-46191-5
    [1. Orderliness—Fiction.   2. Stories in rhyme.]   I. Britt, Stephanie, ill.   II. Title.
PZ8.3.P125My   1993
[E]—dc20   92-36009
                                                               CIP
                                                               AC

Copyright © 1993 by Nancy Hall, Inc.
All rights reserved. Published by Scholastic Inc.
CARTWHEEL BOOKS is a trademark of Scholastic Inc.
MY FIRST HELLO READER is a trademark of Scholastic Inc.

12   11   10   9   8   7   6   5   4   3   2   3   4   5   6   7   8/9

Printed in the U.S.A.   24
First Scholastic printing, August 1993

MY MESSY ROOM

by Mary Packard
Illustrated by Stephanie Britt

My First Hello Reader!
With Flash Cards

SCHOLASTIC INC.

New York   Toronto   London   Auckland   Sydney

I like my room messy.

It's my room. So there!

I like paint
on my table.

I like socks on my chair.

I like books on my bed.

I like toys on my floor.

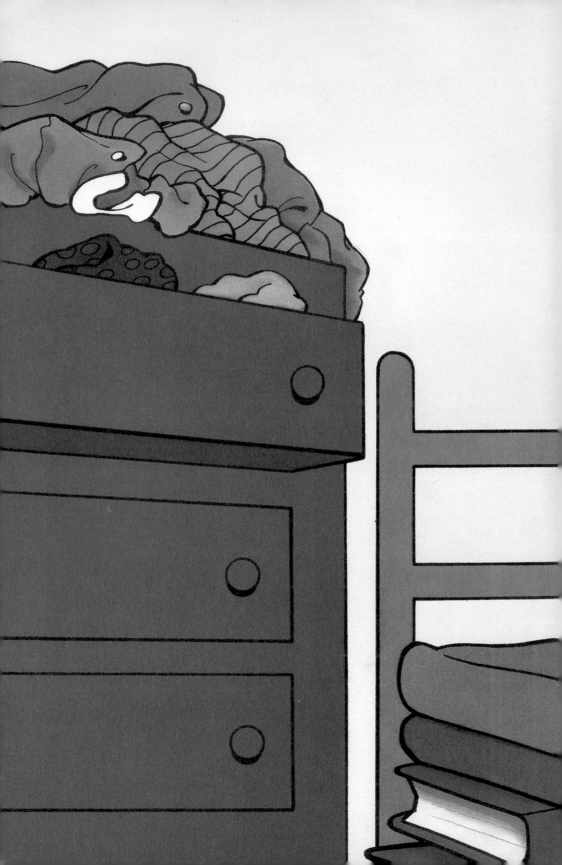

I like shirts
on my dresser.

I like shoes
in my drawer.

I like my room messy.

I like it a lot.
I like it! I like it!

But Mommy does not!

A Very Messy Room

How many things can you find that begin with the letter **s**?

Think About It

The girl in this story feels glad when her room
is a mess. Her mother does not. She feels mad!

What are some things that make you feel glad?

What makes you feel mad?

What makes you feel sad?

What makes you feel bad?

Messy Sentences

The words in these sentences got all mixed up.
Can you put them back in the right order?

messy my I like room

books my like bed I on

lot like I it a

Match Them Up

Use your fingers to match the words in the row on the left with the pictures of these words on the right.

socks

table

chair

shoes

paint

books

bed

Rhyme Time

The word *locks* rhymes with the word *socks*. Can you find words in the story that rhyme with these words?

tie

fair

broom

not

boys

door

Answers

(*A Very Messy Room*)

How many things did you find that began with the letter **s**? Some of these things are:

sailboat, sandwich, saw, saxophone, scarf, schoolbag, scissors, seat, sheet, shell, shelves, ship, shirt, shoe, shorts, shovel, skate, skateboard, sled, slipper, snowsuit, spoon, stamps, stapler, stereo, stethoscope, submarine, sunglasses, sweater

Did you find any other words?

(*Think About It*)

Answers will vary.

(*Messy Sentences*)

I like my room messy.
I like books on my bed.
I like it a lot.

(*Rhyme Time*)

tie / my	not / lot
fair / chair (there)	boys / toys
broom / room	door / floor (drawer)